This book belongs to:

_____

_____

FIVE-MINUTE
Fairy Tales

Cover illustrated by Alessandra Psacharopulo

First published 2017 by Parragon Books, Ltd.
Copyright © 2020 Cottage Door Press, LLC
5005 Newport Drive, Rolling Meadows, Illinois 60008
All Rights Reserved

ISBN 978-1-68052-861-9

Parragon Books is an imprint of Cottage Door Press, LLC.
Parragon Books® and the Parragon® logo are
registered trademarks of Cottage Door Press, LLC.

FIVE-MINUTE

Fairy Tales

Parragon.

Contents

Puss in Boots

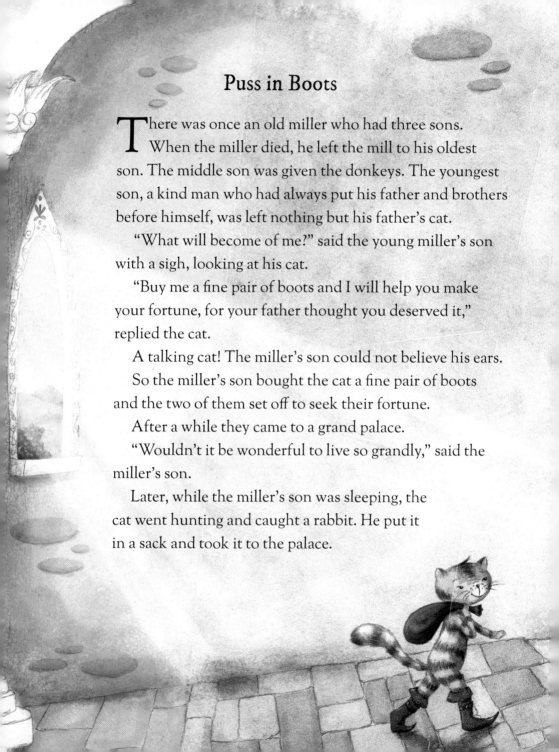

There was once an old miller who had three sons. When the miller died, he left the mill to his oldest son. The middle son was given the donkeys. The youngest son, a kind man who had always put his father and brothers before himself, was left nothing but his father's cat.

"What will become of me?" said the young miller's son with a sigh, looking at his cat.

"Buy me a fine pair of boots and I will help you make your fortune, for your father thought you deserved it," replied the cat.

A talking cat! The miller's son could not believe his ears.

So the miller's son bought the cat a fine pair of boots and the two of them set off to seek their fortune.

After a while they came to a grand palace.

"Wouldn't it be wonderful to live so grandly," said the miller's son.

Later, while the miller's son was sleeping, the cat went hunting and caught a rabbit. He put it in a sack and took it to the palace.

"A gift to the king from my master, the Marquis of Carabas," said the cat, presenting it to the king.

The cat went back to the miller's son and told him what he had done.

"Now the king will want to know who the Marquis of Carabas is," laughed the cat.

A clever cat! The miller's son could not believe his ears.

Every day for a week, the cat delivered a gift to the king, each time saying it was from the Marquis of Carabas. After a while, the king became very curious and decided he'd like his daughter to meet this mysterious nobleman, whoever he might be.

When the cat heard that the king and his daughter were on their way, he wasted no time.

"You must take off all your clothes and stand in the river," the cat told his master.

The puzzled miller's son did as he was told and the cat hid his master's tattered old clothes behind a rock.

When the cat heard the king's carriage approaching, he jumped onto the road and begged for help.

"Your gracious majesty," said the cat, "my master was robbed of all his clothes while he was bathing in the river."

The king gave the miller's son a suit of fine clothes to wear.

"Please join us in the carriage," said the king.

So the cat opened the door and the miller's son climbed in. He looked very handsome in his new suit. The king's daughter fell in love with him at once.

The cat ran on, cutting through the surrounding countryside. Every time he met people working in the fields, he told them, "If the king stops to ask who owns this land, you must tell him it belongs to the Marquis of Carabas."

Beyond the fields, the cat reached a grand castle. He spoke to the people working in a field next to it and discovered that it belonged to a fierce ogre. The cat stood bravely in his boots and knocked on the castle door.

"Who dares to disturb me?" roared a voice from inside the castle.

"I have heard that you are a very clever ogre," called the cat. "I have come to see what tricks you can do."

The ogre opened the door and immediately changed himself into a great snarling lion. The cat felt scared, but he didn't show it.

"That is quite a clever trick," said the cat, "but a lion is a very large creature. I think it would be a much better trick to change into something very small, like a mouse."

The ogre liked to show off his tricks. He changed at once into a little mouse. The cat pounced on the mouse and ate him up.

Then the cat went into the castle and told all of the servants that their new master was the Marquis of Carabas. They were glad to be rid of the fierce ogre, so they did not complain.

"The king is on his way to visit, and you must prepare a grand feast to welcome him," said the cat.

When the king's carriage arrived at the castle, the cat was waiting to welcome him.

"Your gracious majesty," he purred, "welcome to the home of my master, the Marquis of Carabas."

A cunning cat! The miller's son could not believe his eyes.

"You must ask for the princess's hand in marriage," whispered the cunning cat to his master.

The miller's son did as he was told.

The king, who was impressed by everything he saw, agreed.

Soon, the Marquis of Carabas and his wife were married and they lived a very happy life together. The cat was made a lord of their court and was given the most splendid clothes, which he wore proudly along with those fine boots that the miller's son had bought him.

The End

Rumpelstiltskin

Once upon a time, there was a poor miller who had just one daughter. She was very beautiful and he told many people about her.

One day, the king rode through the village. The miller desperately wanted to impress the king. "Your Highness, my daughter is very pretty and smart," he said.

But the king took no notice.

"She can also spin straw into gold!" the miller lied.

"Your daughter must be very clever. Bring her to the palace tomorrow so I can see for myself," demanded the king.

The miller didn't dare disobey the king, so the next day he brought his daughter to the palace. The king led the girl to a room filled with straw. On the floor stood a little stool and a spinning wheel.

"Spin this straw into gold by tomorrow morning, or you will be thrown into the dungeon," said the king. Then he left the room and locked the door.

The poor miller's daughter sat down on the stool and gazed at all the straw around her. She wept bitterly at the impossible task before her.

All of a sudden, the door sprang open and in came the strangest little man she had ever seen.

"Why are you crying?" he asked.

"I have to spin all this straw into gold before the morning, but I don't know how," replied the girl sadly.

"If you give me your pretty necklace, I will spin the straw into gold," said the strange little man.

"Oh, thank you!" gasped the girl, wiping away her tears and handing over her necklace.

The little man sat down in front of the spinning wheel and set to work.

All night long, the little man spun, and by morning the room was filled with reels of gold. And just as suddenly as he had appeared, the strange man disappeared.

When the king arrived, he was astonished to see so much gold.

"You have done very well," he said, "but I wonder if you can do the same thing again?"

He took the miller's daughter to a much bigger room. It, too, was filled with straw.

"Spin this straw into gold by tomorrow morning, or you will be thrown into the dungeon," said the king, and once more he locked the girl in the room.

The miller's daughter was very frightened. The strange little man appeared before her again.

"Don't cry," he said. "Give me your shiny ring, and I will spin the straw into gold."

She handed over her ring gratefully, and the little man set to work. Once again, all the straw was turned into gold.

The king was delighted, and wanted to try one more time.

"If you can do this again, you shall be my queen!" cried the king.

The poor miller's daughter wept even more bitterly this time when the king left.

"Why are you crying?" said the little man, appearing for the third time. "You know that I will help you."

"But I have nothing left to give you," sobbed the girl.

"If you become queen," replied the little man, "you can give me your first-born child."

The desperate miller's daughter agreed to the man's request. And once again, he spun all the straw into gold.

The king was so delighted when he saw all the gold the next day that he kept his promise and married the miller's daughter.

The new queen was very happy and soon forgot about the promise she had made to the strange little man who saved her from the dungeon.

A year later, the king and queen had a beautiful baby boy.

Late one night, the little man appeared in the queen's bedroom as she watched over her sleeping baby.

"I'm here for your baby," he said. "Just as you promised."

The queen was horrified. "Oh, please, take all my jewels and money instead," she begged. "Not my son!"

"No," replied the little man. "You made a promise. But I will give you three days. If in that time you can guess my name, then you may keep your baby."

The desperate queen agreed. The next day she sent messengers all over the kingdom to collect all the boys' names they could find.

That night, the strange man appeared again, and the queen read out the names she had gathered. But after each name he just laughed.

The next day, the queen sent her messengers out to find even more names, and that night she read out the new names when the little man appeared. But once again, the queen's guesses were wrong.

On the third day, the poor queen was in despair. It was getting late by the time her last messenger returned.

"Your Highness, I haven't found any new names," he said, "but as I was returning through the forest, I saw a little man leaping and dancing around a fire, singing a song. It went like this:

"The queen will never win my game,
For Rumpelstiltskin is my name!"

The queen was overjoyed!

When the little man appeared that night, the queen said, "Are you perhaps called... Rumpelstiltskin?"

The little man was furious. He stamped his foot so hard it went through the floor. Then, pulling on his leg until he was free, he stomped out of the room and was never seen or heard from again.

And the king and queen, and their son, lived happily ever after.

The End

Snow White and the Seven Dwarfs

Once there was a queen who longed for a daughter. As she sat sewing by her window one winter's day, she pricked her finger on the needle. Three drops of blood fell from her finger, and she thought, "I wish I could have a daughter with lips as red as blood, hair as black as the ebony of this window-frame, and skin as white as the snow outside."

Before long she gave birth to a beautiful baby daughter with blood-red lips, ebony hair, and skin as white as snow.

"I will call you Snow White," whispered the queen to her new baby.

But soon after, the queen died and the king married again. His new bride was very beautiful, but also very vain. She had a magic mirror and every day she would look into it and ask:

"Mirror, mirror, on the wall,
Who is the fairest of them all?"

And the mirror would reply:

**"You, O Queen,
are the fairest of them all."**

As Snow White became more
beautiful with every day that passed,
her stepmother became more and more
jealous. One day she asked the mirror:

**"Mirror, mirror, on the wall,
Who is the fairest of them all?"**

And the mirror replied:

**"You, O Queen, are fair, it's true,
But young Snow White
is fairer than you."**

When the queen heard these words she was furious.
She called for her huntsman.

"Take Snow White into the forest and kill her!" she commanded.

The huntsman had to obey his queen. He led the beautiful girl
deep into the forest. When he pulled out his knife, Snow White
was very afraid and started to cry.

"Please, don't hurt me," she begged.

The huntsman took pity on her and decided to let her go.

"You must run as far from here as you can," he told her.

Snow White fled into the forest.

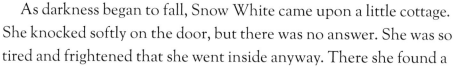

As darkness began to fall, Snow White came upon a little cottage. She knocked softly on the door, but there was no answer. She was so tired and frightened that she went inside anyway. There she found a table laid with seven places and a bedroom with seven little beds. Snow White lay down on the seventh bed and fell fast asleep.

She awoke to find seven little men all staring at her in amazement.

"Who are you?" she asked.

"We are the seven dwarfs who live here," said one of the little men. "We work in the mines all day. Who are you?"

"I am Snow White," she replied.

When she told the dwarfs her story, they were horrified.

"You can stay here with us," said the eldest dwarf.

So every day, the seven dwarfs went off to work and Snow White stayed at the cottage and cooked and cleaned for them.

"Do not open the door to anyone," they told her as they left each morning, worried that the wicked queen would try to find her.

Meanwhile, the wicked queen asked her mirror:

> **"Mirror, mirror, on the wall,**
> **Who is the fairest of them all?"**

And the mirror replied:

> **"You, O Queen, are fair, it's true,**
> **But Snow White is still fairer than you.**
> **Deep in the forest with seven little men,**
> **Snow White is living in a cozy den."**

The wicked queen was furious and vowed that she would kill Snow White herself. She added poison to a juicy apple then disguised herself as a peddler woman and set off into the forest.

"Who will buy my fresh apples?" the wicked queen called out as she knocked at the door of the dwarfs' cottage. Snow White loved apples, but remembered that she must not open the door to anyone. Instead, she opened the window to take a look. When the peddler woman offered her an apple, she was nervous.

"There's no need to be frightened," said the disguised queen. She placed the apple in Snow White's hand. Snow White hesitated, then took a bite. The poison worked the moment it touched Snow White's beautiful red lips. The piece of apple became stuck in her throat and she fell down to the ground.

When the seven dwarfs returned that evening, they were heartbroken to find that their beloved Snow White was dead. Such was their grief that they could not bear to bury her. The dwarfs made a glass coffin for Snow White and placed it in the forest, where they took turns watching over it.

One day, a prince rode by.

"Who is this beautiful girl?" asked the prince.

The dwarfs told the prince Snow White's sad story and the prince wept.

"Please let me take her away," begged the prince. "I promise I will watch over her."

The dwarfs could see how much the prince loved Snow White, so they agreed to let her go.

As the prince's servants lifted the coffin, they lost their grip. The fall jolted the piece of poisoned apple from Snow White's throat and she came back to life.

When Snow White saw the handsome
prince, she fell deeply in love with him.
"Will you marry me?" asked the prince.
Snow White happily agreed.
Before long, the couple were married. The
dwarfs joined them in the prince's castle and they
all lived happily together for the rest of their lives.

The End

The Elves and the Shoemaker

There was once a shoemaker who lived with his wife. Although they worked from dawn until dusk, they were very poor.

"We have only enough leather to make one more pair of shoes to sell," the shoemaker told his wife one day.

"What will become of us?" asked the shoemaker's wife. "How can we live without money?"

The shoemaker shook his head sadly. He cut out the leather and left it on his workbench, ready to start work the next morning.

Then the couple went to bed with heavy hearts.

In the middle of the night, when the house was quiet and pale moonlight shone into the workshop, two elves appeared. They were dressed in rags but had eyes as bright as buttons. They explored the workshop, balancing on cotton reels and peering into cupboards. Soon they found the leather.

Elves are busy little creatures and so they set to work at once, snipping and sewing. As they worked, they sang:

"Busy little elves are we,
Working by the pale moonlight.
While the humans are asleep,
We are busy through the night!"

By dawn, the two little elves had finished their work and disappeared.

When the shoemaker came to start work the next morning, he could not believe his eyes. There, on his workbench, was the finest pair of shoes he had ever seen.

"The stitches are so delicate," he said, as he showed his astonished wife the beautiful shoes. "I will place them in my window for everyone to see."

Soon, a rich gentleman walked by the shop. He saw the stylish shoes and came inside.

The rich gentleman tried on the shoes and they fit perfectly. He was so delighted that he gave the shoemaker twice the asking price.

"I can buy more leather!" said the shoemaker happily to his wife.

That evening, the shoemaker cut out the leather for two more pairs of shoes. He left it on his workbench for the next morning.

In the middle of the night, the two elves appeared again. They explored the workshop, climbing on the tools and swinging from shoelaces. Soon they found the leather.

The elves set to work at once, snipping and sewing. As they worked, they sang:

"Busy little elves are we,
Working by the pale moonlight.
While the humans are asleep,
We are busy through the night!"

By dawn, the two little elves had
finished their work and disappeared.

Once again the shoemaker came
into his workshop and found the
shoes, neatly finished on his bench.
The shoemaker placed them in
his window.

By now, the rich gentleman
had told his friends about the
shoemaker's fine work. The two
pairs of shoes sold that same day for
more money than the shoemaker
could ever have dreamed of. The
shoemaker now had enough money
to buy leather to make four new pairs
of shoes.

"But who can be helping us?" asked
the shoemaker's wife.

That evening, the shoemaker cut
out the leather for four more pairs of
shoes. He left it on his workbench as
usual. Then, the shoemaker and his
wife hid and waited.

In the middle of the night, they watched in amazement as the two little elves appeared. As usual, the elves explored the workshop. They danced with colorful ribbons and juggled pretty beads. Soon they found the leather. Again, the elves set to work, snipping and sewing. As they worked, they sang:

"Busy little elves are we,
Working by the pale moonlight.
While the humans are asleep,
We are busy through the night!"

By dawn, the two little elves had finished their work and disappeared.

"We must repay our little helpers for their kindness," said the shoemaker to his wife.

The couple thought hard about what they could do to thank the elves.

"They were dressed in rags," said the shoemaker's wife. "Why don't we make them some fine new clothes?"

Although they were now very busy in their shop, the shoemaker and his wife spent every spare moment they had making their gift for the elves. They cut out fine cloth and leather, and sewed tiny seams. Soon they had made two little pairs of trousers, two smart coats, two sturdy pairs of boots, and two warm, woolly scarves. They placed the little outfits on the workbench for the elves to find.

That night, when the house was quiet and pale moonlight shone into the workshop, the shoemaker and his wife hid and waited. They watched happily as the two little elves appeared. As usual, the elves explored the workshop. They made a tightrope from thread and bounced on a pincushion. Soon they found the tiny little outfits. They were delighted! They put on the trousers, the coats, the boots, and the scarves and danced merrily around the workbench.

As they danced, they sang:

> "Handsome little elves are we,
> Dancing by the pale moonlight.
> While the humans are asleep,
> We make merry through the night!"

And then, the smart little elves put on their hats and disappeared. The shoemaker and his wife never saw the little elves again. But the couple continued to make fine shoes for their shop and from that day on they always prospered.

The End

Hansel and Gretel

Once upon a time, there were two children called Hansel and Gretel. They lived in a small cottage at the edge of the forest with their father and stepmother.

Hansel and Gretel's father was a woodcutter. He was very poor and the family didn't have much food to eat.

The day came when there was hardly any food left at all.

"What are we to do?" cried the father.

The stepmother, who didn't like Hansel and Gretel, said, "We must take the children into the thickest part of the forest and leave them there. There are just too many mouths to feed."

"We can't do that!" protested the father, for he loved his children dearly.

"We must or we'll all die of hunger!" screeched his wife. "The children are going, and that is that."

From their bedroom, Hansel and Gretel overheard the conversation. Gretel burst into tears.

"Don't worry," Hansel said. "I'll look after you."

When their parents went to bed, Hansel crept out of the house. All around lay little white pebbles that shone like coins in the silvery moonlight. He filled his pockets with them and then went back to bed.

Early the next morning, the stepmother hurried Hansel and Gretel out of bed.

"Come on, children. We're going into the forest to chop wood," she told them.

With a heavy heart, the woodcutter led his children into the forest. As they walked along, Hansel dropped the pebbles from his pockets onto the path.

When they reached the middle of the forest, the woodcutter said, "Wait here. We'll be back as soon as we've finished chopping wood."

Hansel and Gretel waited all day, but their father and stepmother didn't come back. Soon, it was dark among the thick trees. Gretel was frightened.

"We'll find our way home," Hansel comforted his sister.

When the moon rose high in the sky, the white pebbles that Hansel had left on the path lit up. He grabbed his sister's hand.

"Come on, Gretel, the pebbles will show us the way home!"

When Hansel and Gretel returned, the woodcutter was relieved to see his children again, but their stepmother was furious.

Before long the woodcutter and his family had very little food again.

"Tomorrow we will take the children deeper into the forest. They must not find their way home!" the stepmother cried.

This time, as they were led deep into the forest, Hansel left a trail of breadcrumbs.

When their parents didn't return from chopping wood, Hansel said, "We'll follow the breadcrumbs I dropped on the path. They will lead us home."

But when the moon came up, Hansel and Gretel couldn't see any crumbs. "The birds must have eaten them all!" whispered Hansel.

Frightened and hungry, Hansel and Gretel curled up under a tree and went to sleep, waiting anxiously for daylight.

The next morning, they wandered through the forest. After a while they came to a clearing and a little cottage.

"Hansel, look!" cried Gretel. "That cottage is made out of sweets and gingerbread!"

The children were so hungry they grabbed some sweets from the walls of the house. Just then, the door opened and an old woman hobbled out.

"Come in, children," she said, smiling. "I've got plenty more food in here."

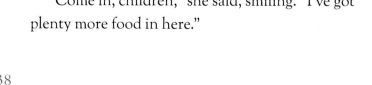

Their stomachs growling, Hansel and Gretel followed the old woman into the cottage. After a delicious meal, she showed them to two little beds and they lay down to sleep.

The children didn't know that the old woman was actually a wicked old witch who liked to eat children!

When Hansel and Gretel woke up from their nap, the witch grabbed Hansel and locked him in a cage. She set Gretel to work cleaning and cooking huge meals to fatten up Hansel.

Weeks passed. Every morning the witch went up to the cage.

"Hold out your finger, boy. I want to feel if you are fat enough to eat."

Hansel, being a smart boy, would hold out an old chicken bone instead. The witch's eyesight was so bad that she thought the bone was Hansel's finger. She wondered why the boy wasn't getting any fatter.

One day, the witch grew impatient.

"I can't wait any longer," she screeched. "I'm going to cook Hansel now!"

Gretel was terrified.

"We'll bake some bread to eat with your brother," said the witch.
"Go and check if the oven is hot enough."

Grabbing Gretel's arm, the wicked witch pushed her roughly
toward the open oven door. Grinning horribly, she licked her
cracked lips. She was planning on eating Gretel too, and couldn't
wait for her delicious meal!

Gretel guessed the witch's trick. "I'm too big to fit in there,"
she said.

"Oh, you silly girl," cackled the witch. "Even I can fit in there."
And she put her head into the oven to prove she was right. Gretel
gave her a giant push and the witch fell right inside. Gretel quickly
slammed the oven door shut.

"Hansel, the witch is dead!" cried Gretel as she unlocked her brother's cage.

As Hansel and Gretel made their way out of the house, they discovered that it was full of sparkling jewels and gold coins. The children stuffed their pockets with treasure.

"Come on, Gretel," laughed Hansel. "Let's go home!"

Their father was overjoyed to see them. He told them that their stepmother had died while they were gone and they had nothing to fear any more. Hansel and Gretel showed their father the jewels and coins. They would be poor no longer!

And from then on, the woodcutter and his children were never hungry again.

The End

Rapunzel

Once upon a time, a young couple lived in a cottage beside a stone wall. They were very poor, but very happy as the woman was expecting a baby. On the other side of the wall lived an old witch. The witch grew many herbs and vegetables in her garden, but she kept them all for herself.

One day the couple had only a few potatoes to eat for their supper. They thought of the wonderful vegetable patch on the other side of the wall. It was full of delicious-looking carrots, cabbages, and tomatoes.

"Surely it wouldn't matter if we took just a few vegetables," said the wife, gazing longingly over the wall.

"We could make such good soup," agreed her husband.

So the young man quickly climbed over the wall and started to fill his basket with vegetables.

Suddenly he heard an angry voice.

"How dare you steal my vegetables!" It was the witch.

"Please don't hurt me," begged the young man. "My wife is going to have a baby soon!"

"You may keep the vegetables – and your life," she croaked. "But you must give me the baby when it is born." Terrified, the man had to agree.

Months later, the woman gave birth to a little girl. Immediately, the witch arrived and grabbed the child. Though the parents begged and cried, the cruel witch took the baby. She called her Rapunzel.

Years passed and Rapunzel grew up to be kind and beautiful. The witch was so afraid of losing her that she built a tall tower with no door and only one window. She planted thorn bushes all around it, then she locked Rapunzel in the tower and never let her see anyone else.

Each day, Rapunzel brushed and combed her long, golden locks. And each day the witch came to visit her, standing at the foot of the tower and calling out, "Rapunzel, Rapunzel, let down your hair." Rapunzel hung her hair out of the window and the witch climbed up it to sit and talk with her. But Rapunzel was very lonely. She longed to leave the tower and to make friends her own age. Each day, she sat at her window and sang sadly.

One day, a young prince rode by and heard beautiful singing coming from the witch's garden. He hid behind a thorn bush, hoping to see the singer. But instead he saw the witch. He watched as she stood below the tower and called, "Rapunzel, Rapunzel, let down your hair."

The prince saw the cascade of golden hair fall from the window and he watched the witch climb up it.

He waited until the witch climbed back down the hair and returned to her house. Rapunzel began her song again.

Enchanted by Rapunzel's lovely voice, the prince climbed over the wall and crept to the tower.

"Rapunzel, Rapunzel, let down your hair," he called softly.

Rapunzel let down her locks and the prince climbed up.

Poor Rapunzel was terribly afraid – she had never seen anyone except the witch before. When the prince explained that he only wanted to be her friend, Rapunzel was delighted. From then on, the prince came to visit her every day. Each time, he carefully waited until after the witch's visit before calling to Rapunzel to let down her hair.

Months passed and Rapunzel and the prince fell in love.

"How can we be together?" Rapunzel cried. "The witch will never let me go."

The prince had an idea. He brought silk, which Rapunzel knotted together to make a ladder so that she could escape from the tower.

One day, without thinking, Rapunzel remarked to the witch, "It's much harder to pull you up than the prince!"

The witch was furious!

"Prince?" she shouted. "What prince?"

The witch grabbed Rapunzel's long hair and cut it off. Then she used her magic to send Rapunzel far into the forest. The girl made her home amongst the animals and birds, and sang sadly as she collected fruit and berries to eat.

Soon, the prince came to the tower and called, "Rapunzel, Rapunzel, let down your hair."

The witch held the golden hair out of the window and the prince climbed up and up and into the tower.

But instead of Rapunzel, he came face to face with the ugly old witch.

"You!" screamed the witch. "You dare to visit Rapunzel? You will never see her again!"

And she pushed the prince back out of the window. He fell down and down, right into the thorn bushes below. The sharp spikes scratched the prince's eyes and blinded him. Weeping, he stumbled away.

After months of wandering, blind and lost, the prince heard beautiful, sad singing floating through the woods. He recognized Rapunzel's voice immediately and called out to her.

Rapunzel ran to the prince and held him in her arms.

"At last, I have found you!" she said, and cried with happiness. As her tears fell onto his hurt eyes, the wounds healed and the prince could see again.

"My love!" he said, and kissed Rapunzel.

Rapunzel had never been so happy. She and the prince were soon married, and Rapunzel's parents came to the wedding. Rapunzel and the prince lived happily ever after in a grand castle, far away from the old witch and her empty tower.

The End

The Nightingale

The Emperor of China once lived in a palace so magnificent that travelers would come from all over the world just to admire it. They returned home and wrote books about the delicate porcelain palace and its beautiful garden where little silver bells were tied to the prettiest flowers and tinkled as you passed by. But most of all they wrote about the Nightingale, with his exquisite voice that brought joy to all who heard him sing.

"How can there be such a bird in my empire, in my own garden? Why has no one told me?" the Emperor exclaimed when he read their accounts.

And he demanded that the Nightingale should be brought to the palace to sing for him.

The palace officials searched high and low for the Nightingale, but without success. At last they found a poor little kitchen girl who told them, "I know him well. Every evening I hear the Nightingale sing. It brings tears to my eyes." And she took them into the forest where the tiny bird willingly burst into song.

The Lord-in-Waiting was mightily impressed and invited the Nightingale to the palace.

"My song is best heard in the woods," the little bird told him humbly.

But when he heard it was the Emperor's wish for him to sing at the palace, the Nightingale went willingly.

There was huge excitement in the palace. The flowers with tinkling bells were brought inside the grand hall and in the middle of the throne room where the Emperor sat, a special golden cage was arranged for the Nightingale.

When his moment came, the little bird sang so sweetly that he melted the Emperor's heart. The Emperor offered to reward him with a golden slipper but the little bird declined.

"I have seen tears in the Emperor's eyes," he said, "I have my reward."

So he was invited to stay at court and was given his own cage. Twelve footmen took him out to fly twice a day and once at night. Each one held a ribbon tied to the Nightingale's leg. The little bird was soon the talk of the land.

One day the Emperor received a mechanical nightingale
encrusted with diamonds, rubies, and sapphires. When it was
wound up, it sang one of the Nightingale's songs, over and over
again. The courtiers soon began to prefer this bird as it sang as
well as the Nightingale but looked prettier with all its sparkling
jewels. So the real Nightingale flew back to his home in the forest.

The artificial bird had its own cushion beside the Emperor's bed and was given the title Grand Imperial Singer-of-the-Emperor-to-Sleep. After a year, every person in China knew the song of the artificial bird and wherever you went, you could hear children singing, **"Zizizi! Kluk, kluk, kluk."**

But then one night, something inside the bird broke. The bird's creator warned that it could only sing once a year from now on, otherwise the music would stop forever.

Five years passed and a real sorrow engulfed the whole country. China's much-loved Emperor now fell ill and the country prepared for a new leader.

"Sing!" the sick Emperor called weakly to the artificial bird. "Sing, my little bird! I have given you gold and precious presents. Sing, I pray you, sing!"

But the bird stood silent.

Suddenly, through the window came a burst of song. It was the real Nightingale. And as he sang, the blood flowed quicker and quicker through the Emperor's feeble body.

"Thank you, thank you!" the Emperor cried. "Little bird from heaven, you have sung away the sadness. How can I ever repay you?"

"You have already rewarded me," said the Nightingale. "I brought tears to your eyes when first I sang for you. Sleep now, and grow fresh and strong while I sing."

"You must stay with me always," said the Emperor. "I shall break the artificial bird into a thousand pieces."

"No," said the Nightingale. "It did its best. Keep it near you. I cannot live in a palace, so let me come as I will. Then I shall sit by your window and sing things that will make you happy. A little singing bird flies far and wide, to the fisherman's hut, to the farmer's home, and to many other places a long way off. I will come and sing to you, if you will promise me one thing."

"All that I have is yours," cried the Emperor.

"You must not let anyone know that you have a little bird who tells you everything." And away he flew.

Early the next day, when the servants came expecting to find their Emperor very sick, they were astonished to hear him speak.

"Good morning," he said, standing proudly in all his fine robes.

The End

Sleeping Beauty

Once upon a time, there lived a king and queen. When the queen gave birth to a beautiful baby girl, the king and queen were filled with joy and decided to hold a christening feast to celebrate. They invited their friends, and all the kings, queens, princes, and princesses from other kingdoms all over the land.

Five good fairies lived in the kingdom, and the king wanted them to be godmothers to his daughter. One of these fairies was very old, and no one had seen her in years or even knew where she was. So when the king sent out the invitations to his daughter's christening, he invited only the four young fairies.

The day of the christening arrived. It was a joyous occasion and the palace was full of laughter and dancing.

After the delicious feast, the four good fairies gave the princess their magical gifts.

Bending over the crib, the first fairy waved her wand and said, "You shall be kind and considerate."

The second fairy said, "You shall be beautiful and loving."

The third fairy said, "You shall be clever and thoughtful."

The baby girl was promised everything in the world that she could wish for. But just as the third fairy finished giving her gift, there was a loud bang, and the palace doors flew open.

It was the old fairy. She was furious because she hadn't been invited to the feast. She rushed over to the sleeping baby and waved her wand, casting a curse upon the child.

"One day the king's daughter shall prick her finger on the spindle of a spinning wheel and fall down dead!" she screeched.

And then she left.

The guests fell silent at these terrible words and the queen burst into tears.

The fourth fairy had not yet given her gift. "Dear Queen, please do not weep. I cannot undo the curse, but I can soften it," she said.

She walked to the crib and waved her wand.

"The princess will prick her finger on a spindle, but she will not die. Instead, the princess and everyone within the palace and its grounds will fall into a deep sleep that will last for one hundred years."

The king thanked the fairy for her kindness and then, to protect his daughter, ordered that every spinning wheel in the kingdom be burnt.

The years passed and the princess grew into a beautiful and kind young woman, just as the fairies had promised.

One day, to amuse herself, the princess decided to explore the rooms in the palace that she had never been in before.

After a while, she came to a little door at the top of a tall tower. Inside, there was an old woman working at a spinning wheel. The princess didn't know that the woman was really the old fairy in disguise.

"What are you doing?" the princess asked curiously.

"I'm spinning thread, dear child," replied the woman.

"Can I try?" said the princess.

No sooner had she touched the spindle than she pricked her finger and fell into a deep, deep sleep.

A strange quietness came over the palace, from the gardens to the tallest tower, and the king and queen began to yawn.

Before long, every living thing within the castle walls had fallen into a deep, deep sleep.

As time passed, a hedge of thorns sprang up around the palace. It grew higher and thicker every year, until only the tallest towers could be seen above it.

The story of the beautiful princess that lay sleeping within its walls spread throughout the land. She became known as Sleeping Beauty.

Many princes tried to break through the thorns to rescue Sleeping Beauty, but none were successful. The thorn hedge was too thick.

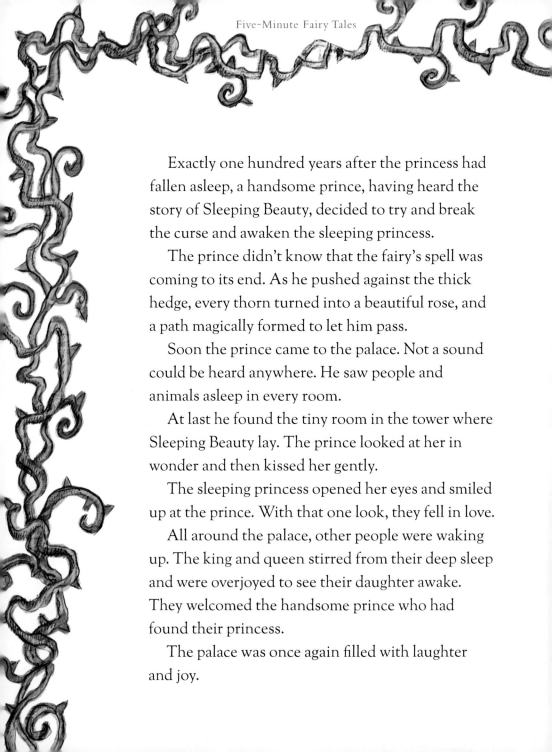

Exactly one hundred years after the princess had fallen asleep, a handsome prince, having heard the story of Sleeping Beauty, decided to try and break the curse and awaken the sleeping princess.

The prince didn't know that the fairy's spell was coming to its end. As he pushed against the thick hedge, every thorn turned into a beautiful rose, and a path magically formed to let him pass.

Soon the prince came to the palace. Not a sound could be heard anywhere. He saw people and animals asleep in every room.

At last he found the tiny room in the tower where Sleeping Beauty lay. The prince looked at her in wonder and then kissed her gently.

The sleeping princess opened her eyes and smiled up at the prince. With that one look, they fell in love.

All around the palace, other people were waking up. The king and queen stirred from their deep sleep and were overjoyed to see their daughter awake. They welcomed the handsome prince who had found their princess.

The palace was once again filled with laughter and joy.

The king called for a huge wedding feast to be prepared, and he invited everyone in the entire kingdom.

Sleeping Beauty married her handsome prince and they lived happily ever after.

The End

The Flying Trunk

Once there was a merchant so rich he could have paved a street in silver, but instead he chose to leave all his money to his idle son. After enjoying the high life, the son soon found that all his father's money had vanished. His friends disappeared, too. But one sent him an old trunk with a note saying, **"Pack up and be off!"**

The merchant's son was amazed to discover that the trunk could fly. So he climbed in, closed the lid, and flew high into the sky, leaving his troubles behind.

At last the trunk descended and he found himself in a foreign land. Hiding the trunk in the woods, he walked into the town.

"Who lives in that palace?" he asked a stranger, pointing up to the hill.

"The king's daughter," came the reply. "It has been prophesied that a man will make her unhappy so no one is allowed to visit, except the king and queen."

Hearing this, the merchant's son had an idea. That evening he flew up to the palace roof and into the princess's room. He was immediately struck by her beauty.

"Do not be afraid," he told her gently. "I am a wise magician descended from the sky."

The lonely princess was excited to have company. She was entranced by the stranger's tales of mermaids in dark blue seas and princesses on magical snow-clad mountains. She believed this magician had been sent just for her and readily agreed to his proposal.

"But first you must come here on Saturday," she told him. "The king and queen will be pleased to hear I am to marry a magician." And then she gave him some advice. "They are exceedingly fond of stories. My mother likes them to be moral and my father likes them to be merry."

"I shall bring a tale as my bridal present," he replied confidently. And before he flew away, the princess gave him a gift of a sabre studded in gold.

"I shall exchange this for more fine clothes," he thought as he waved his princess farewell.

Saturday soon arrived and the
princess proudly introduced her
magician to the king and queen who
invited him to tell them a story.

"There was once a bundle of matches,"
he began. "They lay on a mantelpiece
between a tinderbox and an old iron
saucepan. They often talked about
their youth."

The king and queen smiled
in approval.

The magician continued his tale:

"The matches were proud they were once branches on a fir tree that towered above all other trees. They boasted how the trunk of the tree became a mainmast of a magnificent ship that sailed around the world. And they told how the birds would relate stories of far-off lands they had visited. Which is why the matches felt they were above living in a kitchen."

The queen, who loved a moral tale, applauded when she heard this.

"But where is the merriment?" asked the king.

"Soon," replied the magician, continuing:

"My story is very simple," said the iron saucepan. "I have been rubbed and scrubbed and boiled over and over again. We lead a quiet life here but the newcomer, the turf-basket, tells such terrible tales that the old glass jar fell down in shock and shattered into a thousand pieces."

The king laughed out loud.

"When the jug told her story," continued the magician, "the plates all clattered in applause and the fire tongs began to dance. The kettle was asked to sing but she had a cold so could only sing when she was boiling. Before anyone else could tell their tale, the maid came in to light the fire and struck one of the matches. How it blazed up."

"Now," thought the other matches, "everyone can see we are of the highest rank as we bring a dazzling light."

The king and queen applauded loudly.

"You shall marry our daughter on Monday," the king declared.

The night before the wedding the whole city was illuminated and cakes and buns and sugarplums were thrown to the people in the street.

"I should play my part," thought the merchant's son, so he bought some fireworks and let them off one by one as he flew into the air in his trunk.

The crowd jumped and roared with delight as rockets and fountains of light filled the sky in honor of their princess marrying a magician.

Later, the merchant's son set off into the city.

"I saw the magician," one of the crowd members told him. "He had eyes like sparkling stars and a beard like foaming water."

Happy with his evening's work and excited about his marriage the next day, the merchant's son returned to the wood. But disaster faced him. One spark from a firework had ignited the trunk and it now lay in ashes. The merchant's son could never fly again and could never visit his bride-to-be.

Every day the princess sat on the palace roof waiting for her magician. And he travelled the world telling stories, but they were never as happy as the ones he told at the princess's palace.

The End

Tom Thumb

There was once a poor farmer and his wife who loved each other dearly. But there was one thing missing from their lives.

"How happy I should be if I had but one child," the wife told her husband. "Even if it were no bigger than my thumb, I should love it with all my heart."

So when the wife heard about the great magician Merlin at the court of King Arthur, she persuaded her husband to pay him a visit. Merlin agreed to help and months later the wife had a little boy, no bigger than his father's thumb. They called him Tom Thumb.

Tom was a clever boy and always keen to help his parents.

One day as his father struggled with the cart, Tom had an idea.

"Let me get into the horse's ear and tell him which way to go," he suggested excitedly. So Tom gave the instructions and the horse obeyed.

Watching from the road were two strangers.

"How odd," said one, "that cart is moving and I can hear a voice but can't see anyone driving."

The men followed the cart and soon heard Tom calling, "See father, I did it." And to their astonishment, the farmer lifted the tiny boy out of the horse's ear.

When Tom and the farmer stopped to rest for a moment, the men approached asking if they could buy the tiny boy. They could see he would make them a fortune.

"I'm sorry, but he is not for sale," refused the farmer. "He's my son and his mother and I wouldn't trade him for all the gold in the world."

"Then we will take him from you!" one of them men cried, before the other shoved the poor farmer down a steep hill. They snatched the snail shell where Tom was sleeping soundly and ran off down the road.

Tom was woken by whispering voices he did not recognize.

"There's the parson's house. Let's steal his gold and silver," said one voice.

"But how?" asked another.

"Who are you?" Tom asked, springing from the snail shell. "And where is my father?"

"The farmer didn't want you anymore and sold you to us," said a bald man with a thick beard.

Tom knew this was a lie and quickly devised a plan to elude his captors.

"I can help you rob the parson's house," Tom offered. "I can get into the house without being seen and pass out all the valuables."

The two men were intrigued by Tom's offer and quickly agreed.

Soon Tom found himself standing in the hall of the parson's house.

"Do you want this candelabra?" shouted Tom through the window.

"Keep your voice down," came the whispered reply. But Tom continued to make noise, hoping to wake someone.

It was the cook who woke first. Hearing a clatter and the sound of voices, she sprang out of bed. She failed to notice Tom in the hall but when the thieves saw her at the door, they raced away.

Pleased with his work, Tom crept outside and spent the night in the hayloft.

Early the next morning, the maid picked up a bundle of hay to feed to the cows. Little did she know that she had picked up the tiny boy, too. And soon he was swallowed by a hungry cow.

Tom's cries were drowned out by the loud **"Moo!"** from the cow as she continued to chew the hay happily.

Only later, as the maid finished milking, did she hear Tom calling, "I'm inside the cow!"

The startled maid ran to fetch the parson. It wasn't an easy task, but finally Tom was freed. And yet, his adventures did not stop there.

For just as Tom was crossing a field, he was spotted by a wolf lurking in the trees.

Quick as a flash, the hungry wolf sprang out of the woods and pounced on poor Tom, swallowing him whole. But the clever little boy did not give up. He had a plan.

"My good friend, how would you like a feast?" he called out.

The wolf could not resist. "A feast you say?" he replied eagerly.

"With ham, beef, cold chicken, cake, and every delight you could wish for," replied Tom, directing the wolf to his parents' house.

Arriving there, the wolf headed straight for the pantry. He ate and ate and ate and soon needed to lie down. Inside the wolf's tummy, Tom began to sing very loudly.

"Keep quiet," snapped the wolf, but Tom continued. And his trick worked.

The farmer's wife woke and called her husband. As they peeped into the kitchen, they were horrified to see a wolf sleeping by the pantry door. As the farmer grabbed his axe, he was amazed to hear Tom calling out, "Father, Father! I am inside the wolf."

So the farmer struck the wolf on the head. Minutes later, to the delight of his parents, Tom Thumb was sitting on the kitchen table telling them all about his adventures.

"I have been kidnapped, thwarted a robbery, and been eaten first by a cow and then a wolf," he laughed.

"And now you are home," cried his mother happily. And they all agreed, there was no place better than home.

The End

The Musicians of Bremen

There was once a donkey who worked tirelessly carrying sacks to the mill. After many years the donkey grew weak and his master considered giving him away. One day the donkey decided to run away, setting forth on the road to Bremen.

"I can be the town musician and make a new life for myself," he said excitedly.

When he had gone a little way, he found a dog lying in the road, panting and howling.

"Why are you so short of breath?" the donkey asked kindly.

"Ah," replied the dog. "I am old and getting weaker everyday. I cannot hunt anymore and my master has no use for me, so I left him. But what am I going to do now?"

"I am on my way to Bremen to be the town musician," the donkey told him enthusiastically. "Why don't you come with me?"

The dog happily agreed.

Soon they came across a cat with a face as long as three rainy days.

"Why the sad face, Old Whiskers?" asked the donkey.

"How can I be cheerful?" replied the old cat. "I would rather sit by the stove and purr than chase around after mice. My mistress has little use for me. But where should I go?"

"Come with us to Bremen," the donkey told him. "We can make fine music in the town."

The cat quickly agreed.

Soon the three runaways reached a farmyard where the rooster was sitting on a gate crying out, **"Cock-a-doodle-doo!"**

"Whatever is the matter?" asked the donkey.

"The farmer's wife is going to cook me for supper!" he told them. "So I want to sing while I still can."

"Listen, my red-headed bird," said the donkey. "Join us on our journey to Bremen. You have a pleasing voice and together we can make good music there."

The rooster thought this was a splendid plan.

So the donkey, the dog, the cat and the rooster all set off for the town of Bremen. But they could not reach there in one day.

As evening fell they agreed to spend the night in the forest. The four friends found it difficult to sleep.

"There's a house not too far away," the rooster called out as he spotted a little spark in the distance.

"Then we must go, as there is little comfort here," the donkey said.

"I could do well with a few bones with a little meat on them," agreed the dog, licking his lips.

And soon the four travelers were standing in front of a large house. The donkey, as the biggest, went toward the window.

"What do you see, gray-horse?" asked the rooster.

"Ah," answered the donkey, "I see a table set with good things to eat and drink. There are sparkling jewels and gold piled high." He paused before adding, "And I see robbers, too!"

So the friends planned to drive the thieves away.

The donkey stood with his front feet on the window. The dog then jumped on the donkey's back and the cat climbed on top of the dog. Finally the rooster flew up and sat on the cat's head. And when the four musicians were in place, the donkey called out, "Now, we must sing for our supper."

So the donkey brayed, the dog barked, the cat meowed, and the rooster cock-a-doodle-dooed. Then they all burst through the shutters.

Thinking there was a ghost, the robbers jumped up, screaming, and fled into the woods.

After eating the leftovers, the exhausted friends soon fell asleep.

At midnight one of the robbers crept back into the house. First, he went into the kitchen but it was so dark he didn't see the cat lying on the hearth. He made the mistake of thinking the cat's fiery eyes were live coals and tried to strike a match in front of them. The startled cat jumped up, spitting and scratching him. Then as the frightened robber ran toward the door, he tripped over the dog who leapt up and bit him in the leg.

And his misery did not end there. Just as he was fleeing across the yard, he stumbled and fell on top of the donkey who kicked out in his sleep.

Hearing all the commotion, the rooster woke up with a lively, **"Cock-a-doodle-doo!"**

The terrified robber ran for his life. He was still trembling when he finally reached his friends.

"There is a horrible witch sitting in the house," he told them breathlessly. "She scratched my face with her long fingers. And there is a man standing at the door and he jabbed me in the leg. And a black monster is lying in the yard and it struck me with a wooden club. And there's a judge sitting up on the roof calling out, **Bring the rascal here**."

And from that time, the robbers never returned to the house. But the four musicians of Bremen liked it so much, they never left again.

The End

The Steadfast Tin Soldier

There was once a little boy who was given a whole army of toy soldiers for his birthday. He was bursting with excitement as he lined them all up in their matching red and blue uniforms. Each one had a musket over his shoulder. The last soldier to be made only had one leg as the toymaker had run out of tin. But this one-legged soldier stood just as proud as all the others.

The one-legged soldier admired a pretty ballerina standing in the boy's castle. She was cut out of paper and wore a delicate dress and a sparkling sash. But what struck him most was that she was standing on just one leg.

"She's just like me," he thought, not realising that she actually had two legs.

When the boy marched his soldiers back into their box, the one-legged soldier hid, hoping to talk to the ballerina.

Later, when the boy went to bed, all the toys magically came to life. The jack-in-the-box sprang out of his box, the steam train chugged around, and the ballerina started dancing.

The soldier was entranced.

"She's the most beautiful girl I've ever seen," he said to himself as she twirled gracefully around and around. Just for a moment, he thought she might have glanced his way, too.

"She wouldn't care for you with just one leg!" the jack-in-the-box suddenly hissed, clearly feeling jealous.

Sadly, the soldier realized that the jack-in-the-box was probably right. Why would someone so beautiful and living in a castle care for him? Nevertheless, he still could not take his eyes off her.

"Don't get ideas above your rank," said the jack-in-the-box. "You have been warned!"

The very next morning when the boy came into the nursery he found the one-legged soldier lying on the floor. He picked him up and laid him on the window ledge. A moment later, a gust of wind caught the soldier. He wobbled and wobbled, then fell out of the window.

Down, down, down, he tumbled until he lay on the pavement holding on to his musket.

The boy rushed out to look for him but the soldier was too proud to call for help. As rain started to pour down, the boy went back inside.

"It's true, a soldier should know his place," he thought. "The beautiful ballerina would never be interested in me."

When the rain finally stopped, two boys came out to play.

"Look, it's a soldier!" one cried.

"Let's make him a boat," cried the other.

Carefully folding some newspaper, they tucked the soldier inside and sent him sailing down the gutter.

As the little paper boat rocked from side to side, the soldier held his musket tightly.

Suddenly the boat began to spin and the brave soldier found himself in the darkness of a sewer. He could just make out a pair of glinting eyes ahead.

"How dare you come into our sewer," snapped an unfriendly rat. Soon the brave soldier was being chased by a pack of rats, but just in time, a glimmer of light appeared ahead. The boat was immediately flung into the air before it crashed into the canal and fell apart. As the little soldier sank to the bottom, he still clung to his musket.

"Will I ever see my ballerina again?" was his only thought.

And at that moment a huge fish appeared, jaws wide open. **SNAP!** The one-legged soldier was now deep inside the fish's dark, scary belly. Exhausted, he soon drifted off to sleep.

He was woken by the sound of voices, and then there was a sudden flash of light. Peering down at him was the startled kitchen maid. By chance, she had bought the fish at the market.

"Well I never!" she exclaimed. And, wiping him clean, she took him upstairs to the nursery.

Everyone made such a fuss of the returning traveller.

"Welcome back!" boomed the General. "Tell us about your adventures."

But before he had a chance, the boy burst through the door. He picked up his one-legged soldier and then hurled him into the blazing fireplace.

Everyone thought the boy was being spiteful. No-one realized that the jealous jack-in-the-box had noticed the ballerina gently touch her heart as the soldier returned. He was the one responsible for making the soldier suddenly fly out of the boy's hand. And he was not content to stop there. He then made the nursery door fly open, causing a gust of wind that blew the ballerina into the fire as well. The soldier tried to protect her, wrapping himself around her fragile paper body, but the heat was too great.

By the time the maid came to sweep up, the tin soldier and the ballerina were gone. All that was left behind was a little tin heart, glowing in the ashes.

The End

Cinderella

Once upon a time, there was a young girl who lived with her widowed father. Eventually her father remarried. His new wife had two daughters of her own. She was mean and spiteful to the young girl, and so were her daughters. They made the girl do all the housework, eat scraps, and sleep by the fireplace among the cinders and ashes. Because she slept in the cinders, they called her Cinderella.

One day, a letter arrived from the palace. All the women in the land were invited to attend a grand ball – where the prince would choose a bride!

Cinderella's stepsisters were very excited. Her stepmother was sure one of her daughters would marry the prince. She made Cinderella work night and day to make them as beautiful as possible. Cinderella washed and curled their dull hair. She cut and shaped their ragged nails. She stitched their ballgowns and she polished their dancing shoes until they shone.

Cinderella longed to go to the ball herself, but her stepsisters just laughed.

"You? Go to a ball?" the elder stepsister said. "But you don't have a pretty dress!"

"You? Go to a ball!" laughed the younger stepsister. "How ridiculous! You are always covered in soot and cinders!"

Tears ran down Cinderella's face as she helped her stepsisters into their dresses and jewels. At last they left for the ball. Cinderella sat alone by the fireplace. She cried and cried.

"If only I could go to the ball," she said through her tears, "and be happy for just one night. I so wish I could go."

Cinderella had barely finished speaking when there was a sparkle of light in the dull kitchen, and there stood – a fairy!

"Don't be afraid, my dear. I am your fairy godmother," the fairy said, "and you shall go to the ball!"

Cinderella stared in amazement at the fairy. Quickly, she dried her eyes.

"Really? Can I really go to the ball?" she asked, barely daring to believe it.

"If you do as I say, all will be well," the fairy answered.

"I'm used to doing as I'm told," Cinderella sniffed.

The fairy godmother told her to bring a pumpkin, four white mice, and a black rat. Cinderella hurried to the garden to pick a pumpkin. She found four mice in the kitchen, and she caught a rat sleeping in the barn. With a wave of the fairy's wand, the pumpkin turned into a gleaming golden coach. Cinderella gasped in astonishment.

"It's beautiful!" she said. "But who will pull it?"

The fairy waved her wand again, and the four mice became four handsome white horses. She waved her wand a third time and the rat turned into a tall coachman.

"How wonderful!" Cinderella cried. "But I can't go to the ball in these rags."

"And you won't go in rags!" her fairy godmother laughed.

She waved her wand and Cinderella's rags turned into a beautiful ballgown. Glittering glass slippers appeared on her feet. Cinderella looked lovely!

"Now, off you go," her fairy godmother said, "but remember, all this will vanish at midnight, so make sure you are home by then."

Cinderella climbed into the coach, and it whisked her away to the palace. She had never been happier.

Everyone was enchanted by the lovely stranger, especially the prince, who danced with her all evening. Cinderella enjoyed herself so much that she completely forgot her fairy godmother's warning. Suddenly, the palace clock began to strike midnight.

Bing, bong, bing...

Cinderella picked up her skirts and fled. The worried prince ran after her.

Bing, bong, bing...

She ran down the palace steps. She lost one of her glass slippers on the way, but she didn't dare stop.

Bing, bong, bing...

Cinderella jumped into the coach, and it drove off before the prince could stop her.

Bing, bong, bing!

On the final stroke of midnight, Cinderella found herself sitting on the road beside a pumpkin. Four white mice and a black rat scampered around her. She was dressed in rags and had only a single glass slipper left from her magical evening.

"Even if it was a dream," she said to herself, "it was a perfect dream."

Cinderella

At the palace, the prince looked longingly at the glass slipper he had found on the steps. He could not forget the wonderful girl he had danced with all night.

"I will find her," he said to himself, "and I will marry her!"

So he took the glass slipper and set out to visit every house in the land. At last he came to Cinderella's house. Her two stepsisters tried and tried to squeeze their huge feet into the delicate slipper, but no matter what they did, they could not get the slipper to fit. Cinderella watched as she scrubbed the floor.

"May I try, please?" she asked.

"You?" laughed the eldest. "You didn't even go to the ball!"

"Everyone may try," the prince said. Cinderella sat down. Her foot slipped easily into the glass slipper.

The prince took Cinderella in his arms.

"You're the one!" he said. "Will you marry me? Please?"

Cinderella's stepmother and stepsisters were furious.

"It can't be her!"

"She's just the servant!"

"She dresses in rags!"

But at that moment, the fairy godmother appeared and turned Cinderella's rags back into the fabulous ballgown. Cinderella took the other slipper from her pocket.

"Yes," Cinderella said. "Yes, it was me, and yes I will marry you."

Much to the disgust of her stepmother and stepsisters, Cinderella married the prince the very next day and went to live in the palace. The couple lived long, happy lives together, and Cinderella's stepmother and her daughters had to do their own cleaning, and never went to another ball at the palace.

The End

The Wild Swans

Far away, in a magical land, there lived a king who had eleven sons and a precious daughter, Elise. When their father remarried, the children's lives changed forever. The evil stepmother fed them sand instead of cakes and sent Elise away to be raised by peasants.

Then she cast a spell on the boys.

"Fly away in the form of great speechless birds," she cried. And, at that, the sons changed into white swans with huge flapping wings. They flew out of the windows and far away from the palace.

After many years, the king sent for his daughter. The queen was jealous of the young girl's beauty, so she furiously stained her clothes and skin, and tangled her golden hair. When the king saw her, he cried out, "You are not my daughter!"

Elise wept, and ran far away into the forest. Lost and tired, she lay down to rest. All night she dreamed of her brothers; she missed them dearly. When she awoke, Elise bathed in a fresh pool in the forest, washing away the evil work of the queen.

Elise came across an old woman carrying a basket of berries, and asked hopefully, "Have you seen eleven princes?"

"No," the woman replied. "But yesterday I saw eleven swans with crowns on their heads swim down at the brook."

"My brothers!" Elise cried.

The old woman led Elise to the stream. There, Elise waited until sunset, when at last she spotted eleven wild swans with golden crowns flying toward the land. When the sun disappeared, so did the swans. They transformed into the eleven princes. Elise let out a loud cry of joy as she ran to hug her brothers.

"Every morning at sunrise, we turn into swans," the eldest brother explained. "We spend the day flying and then return to our human form at sunset."

"Please come with us tomorrow, Elise," begged the youngest brother. Elise gladly agreed.

The brothers wove a mat out of willow bark to carry their sister. When morning came, they turned back into swans, and taking the mat in their beaks, they carried Elise through the sky. All day long, they flew across the empty ocean.

Finally, as night fell, they settled down in the fairy kingdom.
As she slept, Elise had a dream that a fairy told her:

"Your brothers can be freed, but only if you weave eleven
shirts out of stinging nettles. Until you have completed the task,
you must not say a word, or else their lives will be in danger."

When Elise woke, she spent all her time weaving the shirts.
The nettles stung her terribly and before long her hands were
covered in blisters, but Elise persevered.

One day as she was sewing, she looked up to find a most handsome king standing before her. When he asked her name, she was unable to speak.

Struck by her beauty, and concerned for her safety, the king reached out his hand, saying, "Come with me."

The king took her to his palace where she was lavished with riches. But Elise could only mourn silently, and the king did not understand why. There were some in the court who were suspicious of Elise, but this did not bother the king, and he married her.

But when Elise was spotted picking nettles from the churchyard, many claimed she was a witch who wanted to destroy the kingdom.

One night as Elise crept out of the chamber, the king followed her to the eerie churchyard where he watched her pick some nettles.

"It is true. She is a witch!" he cried in despair.

The king threw Elise out of the palace, forcing her to sleep among the nettles. But this only delighted Elise, because she knew that she could now finish the shirts for her brothers.

The day came when Elise was taken in a cart to the market square where the crowd was waiting next to a burning fire.

Suddenly, eleven wild swans surrounded her, flapping their wings in desperation. Elise had carried with her the eleven shirts and quickly threw them over the swans.

One by one they turned back into princes but as Elise had not quite finished the last shirt, her youngest brother still had one snow-white wing.

The curse was lifted.

"Now I can speak! I am not a witch!" she cried.

Her brothers surrounded her and called out "She is innocent."

The crowd could hardly believe what they had just witnessed. They now knew this girl was not a witch.

"Forgive me," the king begged.

"Of course," Elise replied.

As the church bells rang out, and the crowd cheered, the king declared he would give each of Elise's brothers a portion of the kingdom.

They ruled wisely and with great kindness, always grateful to their devoted sister.

The End

Little Red Riding Hood

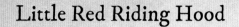

There was once a sweet and happy little girl whose granny had made her a lovely red cape with a hood. The little girl loved it so much that she wore it everywhere she went. Soon everyone became so used to her wearing it that they called her Little Red Riding Hood.

"Little Red Riding Hood," said her mother one morning, "Granny is not feeling very well. Take her this basket of food and see if you can cheer her up."

Little Red Riding Hood loved to visit her granny, so she took the basket of food and set off right away.

"Go straight to Granny's house and don't talk to any strangers!" her mother called after her.

"Don't worry," sang Little Red Riding Hood as she went merrily on her way.

Little Red Riding Hood skipped off through the woods. The sun was shining, the birds were chirping in the treetops and she didn't have a care in the world.

Very soon she met a wolf.

"Well, hello there," said the wolf in a silky, low voice. "And where are you off to on this fine morning?"

"I'm going to visit my granny," replied Little Red Riding Hood, forgetting her mother's warning. "She's feeling poorly and I'm taking her this food to make her better."

The wolf licked his lips.

"Where does your dear old granny live?" asked the wolf.

"She lives in a cottage on the other side of the woods," replied Little Red Riding Hood. "It has pretty roses growing around the door."

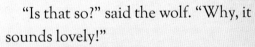

"Is that so?" said the wolf. "Why, it sounds lovely!"

There were some beautiful wild flowers growing in the woods and Little Red Riding Hood stopped to admire them.

"Why don't you pick a pretty posy for your granny?" suggested the wolf.

Little Red Riding Hood thought that was a good idea and stooped down to pick some. As she was busy choosing the prettiest flowers, the wolf strolled away down the path. His tummy rumbled loudly. At the end of the path, he saw a cottage with roses growing around the door, just as Little Red Riding Hood had said.

The wicked old wolf knocked on the door. "Come right in, my darling," called the grandmother, thinking that it was Little Red Riding Hood.

The wolf entered the cottage and before Grandmother had a chance to call for help, the wicked creature opened his huge jaws and swallowed her whole! Then he climbed into her bed, pulled the covers up under his chin, and waited.

Soon, Little Red Riding Hood reached her granny's house with her basket of food and a beautiful bunch of wild flowers.

"Won't Granny be pleased to see me!" she thought, as she knocked on the door.

"Come right in, my darling," replied a strange, croaky voice.

"Poor Granny," thought Little Red Riding Hood. "She doesn't sound at all well!"

Little Red Riding Hood looked in the kitchen, but her granny wasn't there. She looked in the sitting room, but her granny wasn't there either. Finally she went into her granny's bedroom, and she gasped in surprise.

"Granny," exclaimed Little Red Riding Hood. "Your ears are absolutely enormous!"

"All the better to hear you with, my dear," replied a low, silky voice.

"And your eyes are as big as saucers," gulped Little Red Riding Hood.

"All the better to see you with," replied a rumbling, growly voice.

"And your teeth are so...pointed!" gasped Little Red Riding Hood.

"All the better to **EAT** you with!" snarled a loud, hungry voice.

The wicked old wolf leaped out of bed and gobbled up Little Red Riding Hood in one big **GULP!** Then he lay down on the bed and fell fast asleep.

Luckily, a woodcutter was working nearby, and he heard some very loud and growly snoring sounds coming from the little cottage.

"I don't like the sound of that!" he thought. With his axe at the ready he crept into the grandmother's house. He tiptoed into the bedroom and found the wolf fast asleep...with his bulging tummy fit to burst!

"You wicked old wolf!"
cried the woodcutter.
"What have you done?"
He tipped the wolf
upside-down and shook
him as hard as he could.
Out fell a very dazed Little
Red Riding Hood, followed
by her poor old granny.

"It was so dark in there!" cried the little girl. "Thank you for saving us!"

But Little Red Riding Hood's granny was **FURIOUS!** She chased the wolf out of her bedroom, through the cottage, and out into the woods. The woodcutter and Little Red Riding Hood followed close behind her.

The wolf never returned, and
Little Red Riding Hood never
spoke to strangers ever again.

The End

The Frog Prince

There was once a princess with a smile more dazzling than the sun. She lived with her father, the king, in a palace surrounded by thick woods.

When the weather was very hot, the princess would walk into the shade of the forest and sit by a pond. There she would take out her favorite toy, a golden ball that her father had given her. Over and over, she would throw it up into the air and catch it again.

One day, the ball slipped from her hand and fell into the pond with a **SPLASH!** The pond was so deep that she couldn't see the bottom.

"My beautiful golden ball," sobbed the princess. She cried as if her heart would break, her tears drip-dropping into the water. The princess thought her favorite toy was lost forever.

An ugly, speckled frog popped his head out of the water. "Why are you crying?" he asked.

"I have dropped my precious golden ball into the water," she cried.

"What will you give me if I fetch it back for you?" asked the frog.

"You may have my jewels and pearls. Even the crown on my head," sobbed the unhappy princess.

"I don't need any of those things," said the frog. "If you promise to care for me and be my friend, let me share food from your plate and sleep on your pillow, then I will bring back your golden ball."

"I promise," said the princess, but she didn't really mean it. As the frog swam down into the murky water, she thought, "He's only a silly old frog. I won't have to do any of those things."

When the frog swam back up with the ball, she snatched it from him and ran all the way back to the palace.

That evening, the princess was having dinner with her family when there was a knock on the door.

"Princess, let me in," called a croaky voice. When the princess went to open the door, she was horrified to find the speckled frog sitting in a puddle of water. She slammed the door and hurried back to the table.

"Why do you look so frightened?" asked the king. "Was it a witch?"

"No, father, it was a frog," replied the princess.

"What does a frog want with you?" asked the puzzled king.

The princess told her father all about losing the ball and the promise she had made to the frog.

"Princesses always keep their promises, my dear," insisted the king. "Let the frog in and make him welcome."

The princess did as she was told.

As soon as the frog hopped through the door he asked to be lifted up onto the princess's plate so that he could share her food.

When the frog saw the look of disgust on the princess's face, he sang:

"Princess, princess, fair and sweet, you made a special vow
To be my friend and share your food, so don't forget it now."

The king was annoyed to see his daughter acting so rudely. "This frog helped you when you were in trouble," he said. "You made him a promise and now you must keep it."

The princess had no choice. She lifted the damp frog onto her plate and watched as he nibbled at her food.

For the rest of the evening, the frog followed the princess everywhere she went. She hoped that he would go back to his pond when it was time for bed, but he did not.

When darkness fell, the frog yawned and stretched. "I am tired," he said. "Take me to your room and let me sleep on your silken pillow."

The princess was horrified. "No, I won't!" she said. "Go back to your pond, you slimy creature, and leave me alone!"

The patient frog sang:

"Princess, princess, fair and sweet, you made a special vow To be my friend and share your food, so don't forget it now."

The princess had no choice but to take him to her room. She couldn't bear the thought of sleeping next to him, though, so instead of placing him on her pillow, she put him in a corner on the floor. Then she climbed into her bed, laid her head down on the silken pillow and went to sleep.

After a while, the frog jumped up onto the bed. "It's drafty on the floor. Let me sleep on your pillow as you promised," he said.

The sleepy princess felt more annoyed than ever. She picked up the frog and hurled him across the room where he landed with a **SMACK** on the floor. The frog lay there dazed and helpless.

The princess shook herself properly awake and saw the frog lying still. She was suddenly filled with pity. She couldn't bear the thought that she might have hurt the poor thing.

"Oh, you poor darling!" she cried, and she picked him up and kissed him.

The frog transformed into a handsome young prince.

"Sweet princess," he cried. "I was bewitched and your tender kiss has broken the curse!"

The prince and princess soon fell in love and were married. They often walked in the shady forest together and sat by the pond, tossing the golden ball back and forth, and smiling at how they first met.

The End

The Fir Tree

Long ago, in the middle of a forest stood a little fir tree. All around was a wonderful smell of pine and every day the birds sang joyfully. But the little fir tree wasn't happy.

"I wish I was big and tall like you," he complained to all the other fir trees growing high above him. "I wish I could nearly touch the sky and look out over the whole forest!"

"You will be as grand as us one day," one of the other trees chuckled. "Just be patient!"

"And enjoy being young while it lasts," said another. "It's the best time of your life."

"How can it be?" the little fir tree said to himself miserably. "I'm always in the shadows cast by the bigger trees."

Even worse for the little fir tree was the way a cheeky hare kept using him for jumping practice.

"I can leap right over you," the hare gloated as he bounded up to the little fir tree and then jumped easily clear of him. It made the little fir tree so cross.

The little fir tree even envied the big trees that were chopped down by the woodcutters. The birds told him that the trees were carried on horse-drawn carriages and taken to do very important and exciting jobs. Some would become the masts of huge ships and sail around the world.

Two years went by and the little fir tree slowly grew a bit taller. The hare could no longer jump over him now, but still the little fir tree wasn't happy.

"I wish I could be older and taller like other trees," he moaned impatiently. "Will the woodcutter ever notice me and cut me down?"

Next winter, just before Christmas, one of the woodcutters did notice the little fir tree.

"Hmm – what a fine specimen," the woodcutter said as he walked around the little fir tree. "Yes, you will be just perfect."

It hurt a little when the woodcutter swung his axe at him but the little fir tree did not mind at all. At last, he was going to be important.

He wondered whether he was going to be made into a ship and travel the world. Instead, he was taken to a grand house and placed in the middle of the grandest room of all with a very high ceiling. The little fir tree stood tall and proud.

Everyone in the house hurried into the room to admire the tree and the children danced around him gleefully.

He was soon made to feel even more special when the children decorated his branches with baubles, ribbons, and twinkling lights.

How he loved to hear them giggle as they tried to fix a star on his top. It felt as if he was wearing a crown.

And when they had finished, the children joined the adults in singing songs they called Christmas carols.

At the end of the evening, before turning off the lights, the mother took one last look at the little fir tree.

"Beautiful!" she said. "Surely the finest Christmas tree ever!"

The little fir tree had never felt so proud.

Early the next morning, the children rushed in to see him. He thought they were going to dance around him again but this time they just grabbed the boxes from under his branches and ripped off the pretty paper.

The very next day, the little fir tree was shocked to hear the servants say, "Time to take this old tree down."

After all the decorations had been removed, the little fir tree was carried up into the cold, dark loft. All he had for company were a few mice, sheltering from the snow outside.

To pass the time, the little fir tree would tell the mice stories about his forest days – the warm shafts of sunlight, the wonderful tickling breezes, and the chattering birds.

He even smiled when telling them about the cheeky hare always jumping over him.

"It was quite fun really," he admitted.

Then one day as spring arrived, the little fir tree was taken out into the garden. His heart leapt because he thought they were going to replant him. But then he noticed that his branches were now brown and brittle, nothing like the lush green they used to be.

"This tree's quite dead, only good for firewood," said the gardener, dragging him toward a crackling bonfire at the far end of the garden.

"If only I hadn't always longed to be old," sighed the little fir tree. He remembered those warm summer days in the forest when the birds sang so sweetly. He thought about Christmas, too.

And the brave little fir tree wished he had enjoyed himself while he could.

The End

The Little Mermaid

Long, long ago, a mer-king lived under the sea with his six mermaid daughters, who all had long wavy hair and sang with sweet heavenly voices.

The mermaids loved their watery world, but they liked to hear the wise sea king tell them stories about the world above the sea.

"Oh, father, tell us about the cities and the trees and flowers!" they would cry.

"When you are twenty-one, my little ones," their father would say, "you can go to the surface and see all these wonders for yourself."

One by one, the sisters got their chance to visit the surface. At last it was the turn of the youngest sister. The little mermaid swam up through the crystal waters to the ocean surface with great joy in her heart.

Close by was a big
ship. She could see
people on the deck throwing a
party for the prince who was on board.

The little mermaid couldn't keep her eyes off the handsome prince.
As she swam closer for a better look, the sea started to swell and a
strong wind whipped up.

"Oh no!" cried the little mermaid. "A storm is coming."

Suddenly, as the ship was tossed from side to side, the prince was
thrown into the churning water. He began to sink beneath the waves
and would have drowned had the little mermaid not dived down to
rescue him.

Swimming close to the land, she gently pushed the unconscious
prince onto the beach. His eyes flickered open for a few seconds and
he smiled before closing them again. As she swam away, she glanced
back at the shore. A group of people had gathered around the prince.
They helped him to his feet and led him away down the beach.

The little mermaid dived beneath the waves and swam back home.

The little mermaid longed to see the prince again. She became so sad that eventually she told her sisters about the prince and how she had fallen in love with him.

"I know where his palace is," said her oldest sister. "I'll show you."

After that, the little mermaid swam to the surface every day. She gazed at the palace hoping to catch a glimpse of the prince.

"Father, could I become human, if I wanted to?" she asked the king one day.

"The only way, my little one," said the king gently, "is if a human falls in love with you."

But the little mermaid could not forget the prince. She decided to visit the sea witch.

"I can make a potion to make you human," hissed the witch. "But I will take your beautiful voice as my payment. If you win the true love of the prince, only then will you get your voice back."

The little mermaid loved the prince so much that she agreed. She swam to the prince's palace and drank the potion. She fell into a deep sleep.

When she woke up, she was lying on the beach dressed in beautiful clothes. Where her shiny tail had been, she now had a pair of pale human legs. The little mermaid tried to stand, but her new legs wobbled and she stumbled on the sand.

As she fell, two strong arms reached out and caught her. The little mermaid looked up. It was the prince! She tried to speak but her voice had gone, and she could only smile at her handsome rescuer.

The silent, beautiful, and mysterious stranger fascinated the prince. He grew very fond of the little mermaid and spent his afternoons with her around the palace and on the beach.

One day, the prince told the little mermaid that he was getting married to a princess.

"My parents want me to do this," he sighed sadly. "But I love another girl. I don't know who she is, but she once rescued me from the sea."

The little mermaid was devastated, but without a voice, how could she tell the prince that she was that girl?

The prince now took walks along the beach with the princess. The little mermaid could do nothing but watch on from afar.

Over time, the little mermaid became more and more jealous as she saw the prince smiling and laughing. But, deep down, she knew his heart didn't belong to the princess.

A few days before the wedding, the prince asked the little mermaid to take a walk with him along the beach.

"Once I'm married, I won't be able to spend any time with you," he told her.

The little mermaid nodded sadly. She had been dreading this happening.

As they walked across the sand, a fierce wind suddenly whipped along the shore. A huge wave crashed over the prince and the little mermaid, washing them out to sea. Without thinking, the little mermaid dived beneath the churning waves and grabbed the prince.

As the prince lay coughing and spluttering on the sand, he stared at the little mermaid.

"You're the girl who saved me before!" he cried. "I remember now."

The little mermaid smiled and nodded.

"I can't marry the princess. I love you," he sighed. "I don't care if you can't speak. Will you marry me?"

The little mermaid had never felt so joyful and, as the prince kissed her, something magical happened. She could feel her voice returning! Bubbling with excitement, she cried out, "Yes, I will marry you!"

The happy couple were married the very next day. The little mermaid's dreams had come true, but she never forgot her family, or that she had once been a mermaid.

The End

Snow-White and Rose-Red

There was once a poor widow who had two daughters, Snow-White and Rose-Red. In her little garden grew two rose trees – one with white roses and the other with red. The two sisters played in the forest in summer and on winter evenings they would listen to their mother's tales as she sat at her spinning wheel.

One snowy evening there was a loud rapping at the door.

"Hurry," called their mother, "it must be a traveler who is lost." But when Rose-Red opened the door, she screamed as she saw a huge great brown bear panting loudly.

"Please do not be afraid," growled the bear. "I'm half frozen and I merely want to warm up."

Immediately, the kind mother ushered the bear in and let him lie by the fire. At first the sisters were wary of the huge creature but by the end of the evening they were playing happily with him.

For the rest of winter, the bear came every evening and the sisters loved to spend time with him. When spring came, they were very sad when the bear told them, "The dwarfs will soon be back, so I must go deep into the forest to stop them from taking my treasure." And he thanked the mother and sisters for their kindness.

As the days grew warmer and longer and the red and white roses bloomed once more, the sisters spent their time playing in the forest. On one hot afternoon, they stumbled across a very cross-looking dwarf. One end of his long white beard was trapped under a heavy log and he was waving his arms frantically.

"Well, do something to help!" he snapped.

The sisters rushed to his side but couldn't shift the log, so Snow-White took out her scissors and cut off the end of his beard. The dwarf was not pleased. Snatching up a bag of gold that he had dropped, he pushed past shouting, "Bad luck to you both!"

Later when the girls were playing by the stream, they were startled by something jumping in the air. They thought it was a grasshopper but it was the old dwarf. He was caught on a fishing line and his beard was entangled in the thin wire. So once again Snow-White and Rose-Red tried to help and this time it was Rose-Red who snipped his beard to free him. And once again the bad-tempered dwarf grumbled. He snatched a sack of pearls that were hidden in the reeds and ran off.

Later that afternoon, the mother sent the two sisters to the town to buy needles and thread, and laces and ribbons. Crossing the meadow they noticed a large bird hovering in the air. As it sank lower and lower, they heard a piercing cry. To their horror, the sisters saw that the eagle had seized the old dwarf.

Taking pity, the two girls grabbed hold of the little man tightly. As they pulled him from the claws of the eagle, the ungrateful dwarf complained, "You've torn my coat, you clumsy creatures." Then he quickly grabbed a sack of precious stones and ran off toward the woods as fast as his little legs would take him.

By this time, the girls were used to his ingratitude and continued on their way into town.

As they crossed the meadow again on their way home, Snow-White and Rose-Red spotted the old dwarf sitting cross-legged in the grass. He was counting all his treasure. Seeing the exquisite stones glisten in the sun, the sisters couldn't help but gasp at their beauty.

"How dare you sneak up on me!" shouted the dwarf angrily.

At that moment there was a loud growl, and a great brown bear with fiery eyes came charging across the meadow. The frightened dwarf jumped up screaming, "Take these two wicked girls. They would be tastier than me."

But the huge bear swiped the cowardly dwarf with his paw. With one blow, the dwarf was motionless. The girls started to run but then they heard a familiar growl, "Snow-White, Rose-Red, it's me. Don't be afraid."

And as he spoke, the bearskin fell off and there before the startled sisters stood a handsome prince in golden robes.

The happy prince returned to his castle and invited Snow-White and Rose-Red to visit him. The two sisters met the prince's younger brother and all four soon became close friends.

Some time later, Snow-White married the prince and Rose-Red married his brother. The girls' mother came to live with them in the castle where she had her own little garden. She planted two rose trees and every year they produced beautiful roses—white and red.

The End

The Princess and the Pea

Once upon a time, in a kingdom far away, there lived a handsome prince. He had loving parents, plenty of friends and lived a wonderful life in his castle. But one thing made him sad. He did not have a wife.

The prince had always wanted to marry a princess. But he wanted her to be clever and funny, and loving and kind. None of the princesses that he met at parties and balls were quite right.

Some of the princesses were too mean, some were too rude.

Some were too quiet, some were too loud.

And some were just plain boring!

So, the prince decided to travel the world in the hope of finding a perfect princess. He met many more princesses who tried to impress him with their beauty, their dancing and their baking...but still none were quite right.

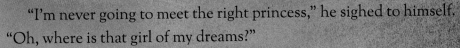

"I'm never going to meet the right princess," he sighed to himself. "Oh, where is that girl of my dreams?"

Months passed without success, and eventually the prince headed back to his castle.

"Cheer up, my son," said the king. "You are still young. One day you will meet a wonderful girl, just like I met your mother." The king smiled at the queen, but he was at a loss to know how to make the prince happy again.

Then one night, when even the king and queen had begun to give up hope of their son ever finding a bride, there was a terrible storm. Thunder roared, lightning flashed, and the rain poured down.

Suddenly there was a loud knock on the wooden castle door.

"I wonder who could be out on such a terrible stormy night?" said the prince. When he opened the door, a pretty young girl stared back at him. She was soaked from head to toe.

"Oh please, Your Royal Highness, may I come in for a moment?" she pleaded. "I was travelling to see some friends, but I got lost in this storm, and now I am very cold and very wet."

The prince ushered the poor girl in out of the wind and the rain.

"You poor thing," said the queen. "You must stay the night. You cannot travel on in this weather."

The prince smiled at the girl. "What is your name?" he asked her.

"I'm Princess Penelope," she replied. "You are all very kind. I don't want to be a bother to you."

At the word princess, the queen smiled to herself. "I wonder..." she thought, but she didn't say anything. She took the girl's hand and said aloud, "Of course not, my dear. Come, and let's get you warm."

Once the princess had changed into some dry clothes, the queen invited her to have some supper with the family.

The prince listened contentedly as the charming princess chatted away over their meal. He could not stop gazing at her. She was clever and funny, and loving and kind. By the end of the evening the prince had fallen in love!

The queen was delighted when she saw what was happening, but she wanted to be quite sure that Princess Penelope was a real princess. She went to the guest room in the castle and placed a tiny pea under the mattress. Then she told the servants to pile twenty more mattresses onto the bed. Then the queen had twenty feather quilts piled on top of the twenty mattresses!

"Now we shall see if you are a real princess!" murmured the queen to herself.

The queen showed the princess to her room and tucked her into the towering bed. "Sleep well, my dear," she said.

In the morning the princess came down to breakfast, rubbing her eyes.

"How did you sleep, my dear?" the queen asked her.

The princess didn't want to be rude, but she couldn't lie. "I'm afraid I hardly slept a wink!" she replied, stifling a yawn.

"I'm so sorry, my dear," said the queen. "Was the bed not comfortable?"

"There were so many lovely mattresses and quilts, it should have been very comfortable," replied the princess, "but I could feel something lumpy and bumpy, and now I am black and blue all over!"

The queen grinned and hugged the girl to her. "That proves it," cried the queen. "Only a real princess would be able to feel a tiny pea through twenty mattresses and twenty feather quilts!"

The prince was filled with joy. He had finally met the princess of his dreams!

Not long after that, the prince asked Princess Penelope to be his wife. She happily agreed and they were married in the castle.

The prince was never unhappy again. And as for the pea, it was put in the royal museum as proof that perfect princesses do exist!

The End

Thumbelina

There was once a poor woman who lived in a cottage. She had no husband but she longed to have a child. One day, she visited a fairy to ask for her help.

"You are a good woman," said the fairy, "so I will give you this magic seed. Plant it and water it, and you will see what you will see."

The woman thanked the fairy and did as she was told. One day, then two days, then three days passed, and nothing happened. But on the fourth day, a tiny green shoot appeared. And on the fifth day, there was a flower bud, with glossy pink petals wrapped tightly around its centre.

"What a beautiful flower you will be," smiled the woman, and she kissed it gently.

With that, the petals unfolded, and in the centre of the flower was a beautiful girl, the size of a thumb. The woman clapped her hands with joy.

"I will call you Thumbelina," she cried, and she laid her new child in a walnut-shell bed with a rose-petal quilt.

Thumbelina was very happy with her mother.

Then one day, while her mother was away, an ugly, slimy toad crawled into the cottage. When she saw Thumbelina sleeping in the bed, she cried, "You'd be the perfect wife for my son!" She grabbed the girl and crept out of the cottage the same way she had entered.

When Thumbelina woke up, she was sitting on a lily pad in the middle of a stream, with two warty toads staring at her.

"This is your new wife!" the mother said to her son. He opened his wide, toothless mouth in a grin, but all he could say was, **"Croak! Croak!"**

"I don't want to marry a toad," said Thumbelina, and she started to cry.

"You ungrateful girl!" the mother toad scolded her. "You'll stay here until you stop crying." The two toads jumped into the water and swam away. Thumbelina sobbed and sobbed.

Then, a fish took pity on her and nibbled through the lily pad's stem until it floated free. Thumbelina sailed gently downstream and escaped from the toads.

At last, she drifted to the riverbank and climbed onto dry land. Suddenly, a big brown beetle grabbed her with his claws.

"Put me down!" said Thumbelina.

"No," said the beetle. "You must stay with me and be my friend."

The beetle carried Thumbelina to a clearing. Another bigger, browner beetle was waiting for him there. He looked at Thumbelina and shook his head.

"Oh, Bertie, she's so ugly," said the bigger beetle. "She can't stay here!"

The two beetles argued and argued, waving their claws in the air, and pulling poor Thumbelina this way and that, until at last Bertie gave in and they let Thumbelina go. She ran off as fast as she could.

Thumbelina lived in the country all summer long. She missed her mother, but had no idea how to find her way home. So she busied herself collecting wild berries and making friends with the birds and small creatures she met.

Then winter came. Thumbelina was cold and hungry and all alone. Luckily, a kindly field mouse found her and invited her to stay with him in his burrow. She was so grateful that she said yes at once.

Life underground was warm and snug, but Thumbelina soon missed the sunshine. And then Mouse's friend Mole asked her to marry him.

"I don't want to marry a mole," cried Thumbelina. "And though I like living with you, Mouse, I miss the sunshine."

"You ungrateful girl!" said the mouse and the mole together. So Thumbelina sadly agreed to marry the mole and a date was set for the following summer.

Thumbelina was miserable. Then one day, as she walked through the underground tunnels, she found a swallow, almost dead with the cold. She hugged the bird against herself to warm him. He slowly opened his eyes.

"You have saved my life," said the swallow. "Come with me to the South, to the land of sunshine and flowers."

"I cannot leave Mouse," sighed Thumbelina, "he has been so kind to me."

"Then I must go alone," said the swallow, stretching his wings, "but I will return next summer. Goodbye!" Then he flew away.

Months passed and the day Thumbelina had been dreading arrived – the day she would marry the mole. As she waited for Mole to arrive, the swallow appeared again.

"Come with me now!" he cried.

"I will!" said Thumbelina.

So Thumbelina flew away to the South with the swallow. As she explored her new home, one especially beautiful flower opened in front of her. There, in the centre, was a fairy prince, no bigger than a thumb, with butterfly wings.

"Will you be my wife?" he asked at once.

"I will!" cried Thumbelina.

So Thumbelina, wearing butterfly wings made especially for her, married the prince and became Queen of the flower fairies. She did not forget her mother, and that very day arranged for fairy messengers to deliver a letter to her and a bouquet of the most beautiful flowers. And kind Thumbelina and her handsome husband lived happily ever after.

The Twelve Dancing Princesses

There was once a king who had twelve beautiful daughters. They slept in one room and every night their father would lock their door. But every morning there were twelve pairs of worn-out dancing shoes under their beds. It was as if the princesses had been out all night dancing. But how could that be? It was a mystery no one could solve except the princesses, and they simply smiled whenever they were asked.

"Any man who discovers the secret of where the princesses go at night," proclaimed the king, "shall have one of my daughters in marriage. But," he warned, "anyone who fails after three nights will be punished by death."

Many suitors tried, but all failed to uncover the secret of the twelve princesses.

Now it happened that a soldier was passing through the kingdom when he met an old woman. Hearing that he would like to be the one to solve the mystery, the woman gave him some advice.

"When one of the princesses offers you some wine," she said, "pretend to drink it and then act as if you are sleeping deeply." And handing him a special cloak, she explained, "Wear this and you will become invisible so you can follow the princesses."

Later that night when the king had locked the door of the princesses' bedroom, the eldest princess gave the soldier a goblet of wine. Carefully pouring it away, he soon pretended to snore loudly.

"We have tricked another one!" laughed the princess as they all changed into their ballgowns and tied their new dancing shoes.

Then as the eldest princess clapped her hands, a trap door magically opened up beneath her feet. One by one the twelve princesses disappeared down the steps. The soldier immediately sprang up and grabbed the cloak. Just as the old woman had predicted, he now became invisible. But in his haste, he stepped on the hem of the dress of the youngest princess.

"Someone has pulled my dress," she cried.

"Don't be silly," replied one of her sisters, "it's just a nail."

At the bottom of the stairs, a door opened out to a spectacular avenue of trees, each one bearing silver leaves that shimmered under the starlit sky.

Following closely behind the laughing princesses, the invisible soldier broke off a silver branch, which snapped loudly.

"See, we are being followed," cried the youngest princess. But her sisters were too excited to worry.

Leaving the silver trees behind, the happy princesses now ran daintily through an avenue of pure gold trees. It was a magnificent sight in the moonlight.

The soldier followed, snapping off a golden branch. Finally they reached the glittering diamond trees and to the invisible soldier, this was the most breathtaking sight of all. As the soldier snapped off a branch from a diamond tree, the youngest princess screamed but her sisters only laughed more loudly as they ran toward the lake. Lined up on the water were twelve little boats and in each was a prince ready to row the princesses across to the castle. The soldier jumped into the boat with the youngest princess as the sound of trumpets filled the air.

Inside the castle, music and laughter rang out as the princesses danced with their handsome princes in the ballroom. The youngest princess was the only one feeling uneasy all evening. Every time she lifted a goblet of wine, it was snatched out of her hand by the mischievous soldier. She tried in vain to warn her sisters but they were only interested in having fun. They danced and danced until finally the cock crowed. Then the twelve princes rowed them back across the lake.

The soldier managed to run ahead and was back in bed snoring when the princesses returned to their room.

"We're safe!" whispered the eldest sister checking up on the sleeping soldier. Happy but tired, the twelve princesses took off their tattered dancing shoes and were soon fast asleep.

The soldier followed the princesses again the next night and on the third night he took a golden goblet from the castle as proof of where the sisters had been. So when he was summoned to the king after the final night, he was able to show him a silver branch, a gold branch, and a diamond branch, as well as the castle goblet. The princesses' secret had finally been discovered. The grateful king kept his promise.

"Which of the princesses will you choose for your wife?" he asked the soldier.

"I am not a young man, sir," replied the soldier, "so I think I will choose the eldest."

Soon they were married and in time the soldier became king of the whole country. He ruled wisely and never forgot the old woman in the woods and her words of advice.

The End

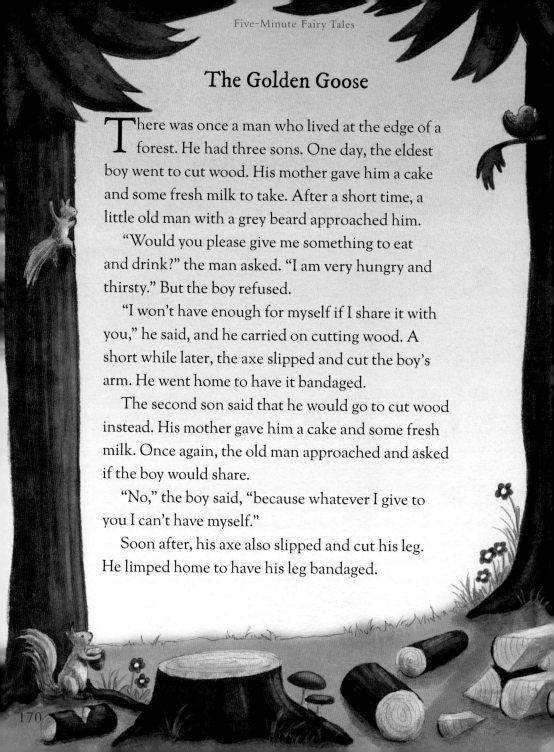

The Golden Goose

There was once a man who lived at the edge of a forest. He had three sons. One day, the eldest boy went to cut wood. His mother gave him a cake and some fresh milk to take. After a short time, a little old man with a grey beard approached him.

"Would you please give me something to eat and drink?" the man asked. "I am very hungry and thirsty." But the boy refused.

"I won't have enough for myself if I share it with you," he said, and he carried on cutting wood. A short while later, the axe slipped and cut the boy's arm. He went home to have it bandaged.

The second son said that he would go to cut wood instead. His mother gave him a cake and some fresh milk. Once again, the old man approached and asked if the boy would share.

"No," the boy said, "because whatever I give to you I can't have myself."

Soon after, his axe also slipped and cut his leg. He limped home to have his leg bandaged.

The youngest boy, Billy, then said that he would go to cut wood. His father refused.

"You are a silly boy. Your brothers have hurt themselves, so you certainly will, too," he said.

But Billy insisted. At last, his mother gave him a dry biscuit and a bottle of plain water and he set off into the forest. No sooner had he started work than the old man appeared and asked for a drink and a bite to eat.

"It's plain food," Billy said, "but if you're happy with dry biscuit and water, I'll gladly share with you."

They shared the biscuit and water, then the little old man said, "You have been good to me, and you will have your reward. Cut down that tree over there and see what you find inside it."

Billy did as the man said. Hidden inside the tree trunk he found a goose with shining feathers of pure gold! Billy wondered how there could be such a strange bird. He looked around for the old man, but he had vanished, so Billy picked up the goose and set off for home.

Before long, Billy was totally lost. It was growing dark, so when he came to an inn he decided to stay the night.

The innkeeper had three daughters. They were very curious about the golden goose. When Billy went for supper, the eldest girl thought she would steal a single feather. As soon as she put her hand on the goose, she stuck fast to it! No matter how she struggled, she couldn't get free.

The middle girl, also wanting a feather, tried to push her sister out of the way, but found that she became stuck fast to her sister's arm.

When the youngest girl approached, her sisters warned her not to touch them. But she thought they were trying to keep the golden feathers all for themselves. She took hold of the middle sister's arm, and immediately she stuck like glue.

The next morning, Billy set off down the street with the golden goose, dragging the girls behind him. As they passed a church, the parson called out, "What are you girls doing, running after that young man? Let go at once!"

He tried to pull the youngest girl away, but he was then as stuck as they were. The parson called to his wife to free him, but that just ended with the wife sticking to the parson.

Two farmers ran from their fields to help the strange group, and soon they were stuck fast, too.

By now there were seven people in a line following behind the boy with his golden goose. It was the strangest procession you could imagine!

It happened that they passed near the king's palace. He had a daughter, but she was always miserable. No one could make the princess smile, let alone laugh. The king was so desperate to cheer her up that he had promised her hand in marriage to anyone who could make her happy. Many young men had tried to amuse her, telling jokes, doing tricks, fooling around, and making faces, but nothing worked – she was as sad as ever.

When the princess looked out of her window that day and saw Billy walking along the street carrying a golden goose, she started to smile.

Then she saw the three sisters, the parson, the parson's wife, and the two farmers staggering along behind. Her smile turned to a laugh and her laugh became louder and louder. She laughed so hard that tears ran down her cheeks.

"My dear, what has made you laugh?" the king cried, delighted. The princess was laughing so much she couldn't speak. She could only point at Billy and the long line of people stuck to the goose.

The king sent a footman to bring Billy to the palace.

"The princess is laughing!" the king exclaimed. "You made her laugh! That means you may marry her!"

"I? Marry the princess?" Billy said.

"Why, yes," the king answered. "I am so glad that at last someone has helped my poor, sad daughter. All I want is for her to be happy – if you can make her smile and laugh, you are the best husband she could have."

Suddenly the golden goose jumped from Billy's arms, and all the people toppled backward, unstuck.

Billy and the princess soon married, and they lived long, happy lives full of smiles and laughter.

The End

The Emperor's New Clothes

Once upon a time, there lived an emperor who really loved clothes. He would strut around his palace in different outfits, day and night. There were mirrors in every room so he could admire his reflection as he passed by.

The emperor had outfits for the morning...

... and different outfits for the afternoon...

... and extra special outfits for the evening made from the most expensive cloth and sewn with pure gold thread.

In fact, the emperor had so many clothes that he often didn't know what to wear!

One day, two wicked men called at the palace. They knew all about the emperor's love of clothes.

"Your Highness, we are weavers," they said. "But we can do something that no other weavers can do. We can make a magic cloth. This cloth is very special because only very clever people can see it."

The emperor was impressed. "I would like you to make me a suit from this magic cloth," he said.

"Of course, Your Highness, it would be an honor," said the first weaver.

"Sire, we will need lots of gold thread," said the second weaver.

"You shall have all the gold thread you need," replied the emperor. He turned to one of his servants. "Please show these fine gentlemen to the royal storeroom."

The two men had never seen so much gold thread. Laughing and clapping their hands with glee, they filled their bags, and left the palace.

A few days later the emperor called for one of his ministers.

"Go and find out how the weavers are getting on," he ordered impatiently. "I need something new to wear."

The minister went off to the weavers' workshop. There he found the two weavers sitting in front of a loom, busy at work.

The minister rubbed his eyes. He couldn't see any cloth on the loom.

"That's strange," he thought. Not wanting to appear foolish, he smiled at the weavers.

"The cloth is looking wonderful. When will the emperor's suit be ready?" he asked.

"Soon, soon," replied the first weaver.

"But we will need more gold thread to complete the suit," said the second weaver.

The minister hurried back to the emperor. As soon as he had gone, the weavers roared with laughter.

"Oh, this is priceless! What a foolish man!"

Back at the palace, the minister bowed before the emperor. Not wishing to be called a fool he said, "Sire, I have never seen a cloth more beautiful. The weavers need more gold thread to finish your suit."

"Well, send more over then," replied the emperor.

For a whole week the weavers pretended to cut and sew the magic cloth to make the new suit. At last they returned to the palace, proudly pretending to carry the cloth.

The emperor was very excited and handed the weavers a bag of gold coins to pay for the outfit. He took off his clothes and the weavers fussed around him, pretending to smooth and adjust the suit.

"It fits you perfectly!" they cried.

The emperor looked in the mirror. He couldn't see any clothes, but not wanting to appear foolish, he said, "It's wonderful!"

As soon as the two men had left the palace, they doubled over with laughter. Their cunning plan had worked.

News of the emperor's suit quickly spread throughout the kingdom. Everyone was sure they would be able to see the magic cloth.

"Yes, Sire, truly splendid!" agreed the emperor's ministers.

No matter how hard he looked, the emperor still could not see any clothes.

"I can't be more of a fool than my ministers," he thought, "and they can all see the suit." So he smiled at the weavers and thanked them once again.

The vain emperor sent out a royal announcement. He would lead a grand procession through the city wearing his new suit.

When the great day arrived, the emperor sent for the two weavers to help him get dressed.

"Ah, Your Highness, you do look wonderful," they cried.

People had gathered in the streets to catch a glimpse of the emperor as the procession passed by. Finally the emperor appeared riding on a fine white horse. Nervous whispers rippled through the crowd. No one wanted to appear foolish, so at last a timid voice called out, "The emperor's new clothes are magnificent!"

Suddenly everyone started talking and shouting at once.

"How stylish!"

"Smart and fashionable!"

The emperor smiled as he trotted along, feeling very pleased with himself. Then a small boy and his sister pushed to the front of the crowd. They started to point and giggle.

"Look!" they cried. "The emperor has no clothes on!"

Suddenly, everyone knew that it was true. Before long the laughter had spread through the crowd.

The emperor turned bright red.

"What a fool I am!" he gasped. "How could I have been so silly and vain?" He looked around for the two weavers, but of course they were nowhere to be seen.

Filled with shame, the emperor made his way back to the palace to get dressed.

"I will never be so vain about my clothes again," said the emperor to his minister.

He was true to his word – and he was a much happier emperor from that day on.

The End

The Ugly Duckling

Once upon a time, there was a proud and happy duck. "I have seven beautiful eggs and soon I will have seven beautiful ducklings," she told the other creatures of the riverbank.

It wasn't long before she heard a **CRACK!** And one beautiful duckling popped her little head out of the shell.

"Isn't she a beauty!" she exclaimed. Soon there was another... and then another... until she had six beautiful little ducklings, drying their fluffy yellow wings in the spring air.

"Just one egg left,"
quacked Mother Duck,
"and it's a big one!" For quite
a while, nothing happened.
Mother Duck was starting to
worry when, at last, the big egg
began to hatch.

Tap, tap, tap! Out came a beak.

Crack, crack, crack! Out popped a head.

Crunch, crunch, crunch! Out came the last duckling.

"Oh, my!" said Mother Duck. "Isn't he…different!"

The last duckling did look strange. He was bigger than the other ducklings and didn't have such lovely yellow feathers.

"That's all right," said Mother Duck. "You're my special little duckling. Now come on into the water," she told her little ones. "You must learn to swim straight away." One by one, the ducklings hopped into the water, landing with a little plop. But the ugly duckling fell over his big feet and landed in the water with a great big **SPLASH!** The other ducklings laughed at their clumsy brother.

"Now, my little chicks," said Mother Duck, "stick together and stay behind me!"

Back at the nest, the ducklings practiced their quacking.

"Repeat after me," said their mother. "Quack, quack, quackety-quack!"

"Quack, quack, quackety-quack!" repeated the ducklings, all except for the ugly one.

"Honk! Honk!" he called. However much he tried, he couldn't quack like his brothers and sisters.

"What a racket!" said Mother Duck. "I'm sure you'll get the hang of it soon enough."

The other ducklings all quacked with laughter.

The ugly duckling hung his head in shame.

"Nobody likes me," he thought. "I'll never fit in."

The next day, the mother duck took her little ones out for another swim. Once again, the little ducklings stayed close to her while the ugly duckling wandered alone. Some wild geese came swooping down and landed on the river nearby.

"What kind of a bird are you?" asked one goose, rather rudely.

"I'm a duckling, of course," he replied. "My family have left me all alone."

The rest of the geese felt sorry for the ugly duckling.

"Come away with us," they said. "It's a big wide world and there's so much to see!" But the ugly duckling was afraid to leave his river, so he stayed where he was.

When their mother wasn't looking, the other ducklings teased their ugly brother.

"Just look at his dull, grey feathers," said his sister unkindly, as she admired her own reflection in the water. "Mine are so much prettier!"

The ugly duckling swam away and looked at his reflection.

"I don't look the same as them," he thought.

Feeling sad and lonely, he swam down the river and didn't stop until he'd reached a place he had never seen before. "I may as well stay here by myself," he decided.

Summer turned to autumn. The sky became cloudy and the river murky. But still the ugly duckling swam alone in his quiet part of the river.

Snow fell heavily that winter and the ugly duckling was cold and lonely. The river was frozen solid.

"At least I can't see my ugly reflection any more," he thought to himself.

Spring arrived at last and the ice thawed. New visitors arrived on the river. The ugly duckling watched nervously as some magnificent white ducks swam toward him.

"You're very big ducks," he told them, when they swam close.

"We're not ducks," laughed the elegant creatures. "We're swans – just like you!"

The ugly duckling didn't know what they meant. He looked at his reflection in the river and was surprised to see beautiful white feathers and an elegant long neck.

"Is that really me?" he asked, surprised.

"Of course it is," they told him. "You are a truly handsome swan!"

The handsome young swan joined his new friends and glided gracefully back up the river with them.

When he swam past a family of ducks, Mother Duck recognized her ugly duckling right away.

"I always knew he was special," she said.

And the beautiful young swan swam down the river proudly, ruffling his magnificent white feathers and holding his elegant head high.

The End

Index